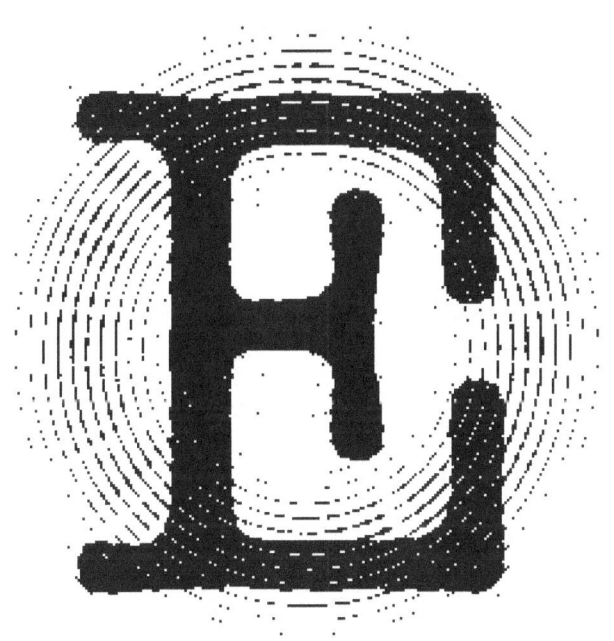

Enigmatic Ink - Canada

First Paperback Edition 2014
Published Simultaneously in Canada and the US

Enigmatic Ink, London, Canada
www.enigmaticink.com

ISBN: 978-1-926617-22-0

Cover artwork Ustrojenstvozagyvat III, 2013, Copyright © M S Waldron
Matthew Waldron is also the experimental sound artist known as
irr. app.(ext.)
http://irrappext.com

"Eat the Word" was first published in *Paroxysm* by Paroxysm Press, Adelaide, 1998. www.paroxysmpress.com

EAT THE WORD

Enigmatic Ink: London, Canada

CONTENTS

FOREWORD..8

EAT THE WORD 11

LIQUID CONVULSIVE...17

PLASTICINE..21

VIDEO GAMES..24

KUN(S)T 27

DEFACED CELL 35

UNMANNED 40

WALL 43

DÉFÉNESTRE 47

"May it please heaven that the reader, emboldened and having for the time being become as fierce as what he is reading, should, without being led astray, find his rugged and treacherous way across the desolate swamps of these sombre and poison-filled pages; for, unless he brings to his reading a rigorous logic and a tautness of mind equal at least to his wariness, the deadly emanations of this book will dissolve his soul as water does sugar. It is not right that everyone should read the pages which follow; only a few will be able to savour this bitter fruit with impunity. Consequently, shrinking soul, turn on your heels and go back before penetrating further into such uncharted, perilous wastelands. Listen well to what I say: turn on your heels and go back, not forward, like the eyes of a son respectfully averted from the August contemplation of his mother's face...."[1]

Notes

1   Comte de Lautreamont (Isidore Ducasse) *Maldoror* London,
     Penguin Books, 1978, P. 29.

FOREWORD

Of Frames and Flames

How does one curate lines of escape if by escape we mean literary thought that is both on and beyond limit? Curation must fix upon coordinates of space-time, freezing processes into states, landmarks, objects, and artifacts. It must pin them down, secure them in vitrines, and affix pithy explanatory notes so that it conforms to the discursive order or set to which the work belongs. Escapism is a misnomer, for escapism contains in itself the very rules that ameliorate all forms of movement, subjecting them to the solidifying gaze. It is less an actual escape, than it is exotic transport from one point on a line segment to the next. However, as Lort so exquisitely recognizes in "DÉFÉNESTRE," "The fall is the passage of escape, the passage of sensation, the most intense and radical departure. Folding the line to the outside, folding it back inside, curled around, out manoeuvred, stretched till it breaks." It is here that the reference splits between the passage of work and the passage of life as pure flows and intensities, and even in these vignettes - for lack of a better term - there is certainly an extension to the limit, and that by way of the great disequilibrium that allows for the discharge of a foreign language within the language [Deleuze 112]. This is the outside of the presentation case, the pedestal, the frame, but the limit - and by the deviant descent that marks it in pure sense - is enclosed by the release or fall of the language itself: the painting consumes the frame, and the once stable categorical and taming order of the parergon [what Kant designates as the frame that contains the work] is no longer what comes to define the work as a work, nor is it the supplements and adornments of the statue, but all is rolled up and outward in this tumbling cascade.

Lort's literary offerings, this bundle or ensemble of disparate texts that do share a zone or neighbourhood of concepts in a Deleuzo-Guattarian sense, owes a major debt precisely to the thought of Deleuze and Guattari - but not slavishly so. An apprenticeship is not a repetition or a scene of imitative reproduction, but an inspirational line, an arc or vector that emerges from an initial condition to produce a differentiating turbulence. It is this unstable vector that inscribes the very limit of the language, allowing it to devolve upon itself and even commit its own act of autophagy.

I've been tossed along on a decade's worth of Lort's escapes, or rather, that his archipelago of writings which contain both literary and theoretical flora and fauna result in a reader performing an act of island-hopping. There are moments of convulsion, of being held hostage by the linguistic frame, of the dramatic tension when the hostage is set free by main force. But in reading a decade of Lort, the most uninteresting and trivial of questions to answer, as is far too common in assessing the corpus of an author, is the dogmatic "maturation of the author" which attempts to trace a linear, upward trending line to show "development" that obscures difference. When writing is reduced to the narrow constraints of a modular, progressive mastery through practice, this assumes a telos, an apogee being reached that conforms to a kind of Royal Science of writing. Lort has not written "better" over this past decade; he has written differently.

Logophage
In Nietzschean terms, one must have the strongest of constitutions to eat the word, for it is also to masticate the hard and stale grit of the order-word, the redundancies of that order: "an order always and already concerns prior orders, which is why ordering is redundancy." [Deleuze and Guattari 75]. The infinite chain of signifiers, the regime of signs, is the tapeworm in the gut of language, draining it of nutrients, causing the reverse to flow from it in emission, which the good reader or writer understands must not be contained inside in some perversion of Protestant noble suffering. No, it must form part of the great Ekel Nietzsche advocates: that grand act of disgust and violent discharge that - like Jubal Brown on a priceless and culture industry relic Mondrian - discharges that disgust in a moment that can only be captured in the present as an act of situational resistance. What one digests, and chooses to keep in the abdomen of language, are the incorporeal transformations. Upon the tiled floor of modernism is the vomit of disgust.

You are what you eat. If a text "is caught up in a system of references to other books, other texts, other sentences: it is a node within a network" [Foucault 23]. In S/Z Barthes tells us that the ideal text is composed of networks that

> are many and interact, without any one of them being able to surpass the rest; this text is a galaxy of signifiers, not a structure of signifieds; it has no beginning; it is reversible; we gain access to it by several entrances, none of which can be authoritatively declared to be the main one; the codes it mobilizes extend as far as the eye can reach, they are indeterminable [5].

Rejecting what Baudrillard would call the "promiscuity of networks" in what contains the heavily saturated tracing patterns of communication theory since cybernetics and Claude Shannon with its binary sender-receiver assumptions, Lort's prose-poems of sense [in the Deleuzian register of that term] creates an island chain that allow for floating elements, floating signifiers: "What are texts? Strings of differential traces. Sequences of floating signifiers. Sets of infiltrated signs dragging

9

along ultimately indecipherable intertextual elements"(Leitch, 122).

The literary text is a play of textuality, not simply in the obvious sense that a "work" of art always originates in the historical field of predecessors. Its own play of difference mirrors its displacement and reappropriation of other texts, and anticipates the necessary critical text which must "supplement" it. (Riddel 589)

Lort presents us with a conspicuous form of the literary economy, his own version of a Bataillean "accursed share":

> With its bloated eyes squinting the dog excretes out from its arse, what appears to be a page onto the floor. At once the girl snatches up the page. She recognizes it as one of the pages from the book that she had fed the dog, only the words have been rearranged, crapped out and skew-whiffed.

It is this act of the consumption, digestion, and processing that produces the "remainder" that cannot be retained. It is a production, but one that is predicated on the discharge of what cannot be held inside. It leaves wide open the question of this very book: are we, the readers, privy to the inside of language's guts, or the defecatory remainder of what could not be contained inside. And, we might ask if we must perform a kind of de Sade inspired coprophagic act in also consuming these printed matters, and cycling them through our own systems. If so, then this book may certainly inspire our own productions in like fashion, creating a new vector or chain of consumption and evacuation. Do we, the readers, have the constitution for such reconstitution, productions which will always produce the different?

Kane X. Faucher
London, 2014

Barthes, R. [1990]. *S/Z*. Trans. Richard Miller. London: Blackwell.

Deleuze G. [1997`]. "He Stuttered." *Essays Critical and Clinical*. Trans. Daniel W. Smith and Michael A. Greco. Minneapolis: University of Minnesota Press.

Deleuze, G., and F. Guattari [1987]. *A Thousand Plateaus*. Trans. Brian Massumi. Minneapolis: University of Minnesota Press.

Foucault, M. [1972]. *The Archaeology of Knowledge*. Trans. A.M. Sheridan Smith. New York: Pantheon Books

Leitch, V. B. [1983]. *Deconstructive Criticism: An Advanced Introduction*. New York: Columbia University Press.

Riddel, J. N. [1976]. "From Heidegger to Derrida to Chance: Doubling and (Poetic) Language." *Boundary 2*, 4.2: 569-592.

EAT THE WORD

"I am the only child left in the world," she says smirking with an irrepressible grin, which dilates the features of her small ungainly face. She rests her limbs on top of the metal railing and looks out over the deserted vastness that surrounds her high rise apartment block. The expanse is dead with silence. An icy wind caresses over the cool skin of her young face, lifting her straggly uncombed lengths of brownish hair into a flutter that twirls in leaps and eddies. She watches as an unhinged door is swept awkwardly down an avenue, until it merges out of sight. A dishevelled and unfed bird, seemingly having noticed the girl, perches itself on the railing a short distance from the girl. The girls attention moves to the bird. The bird's body shivers, small droplets of water cling to the edges of its black feathers and a thin crust of ice attaches itself to its beak. The birds reddish eyes stare longingly at the girl in a similar visual scrutinising. Periodically the bird ruffles its feathers seemingly as an effort to prevent the moisture from seeping inward. The bird's spindly legs momentarily slip on the icy wet surface of the railing. The girl giggles as the ravenous bird regains its balance. The febrile bird adjusts its position, siting hunched up, with its belly resting on the railing. The bellowing wind whines out its familiar howling reverberation. In the distance, enclosed between a horizon and a ragged stretch of coastline, a gray dead ocean heaves and sighs in its cold misery.

The girl turns away and goes back inside. The dark shadows swell as they swallow and lick her body. The black bird clambers along the railing almost calling her back. At once the immense heat of the room hits her in the face. Almost spontaneously her brow becomes moist with sweat. The heat radiates onto her body, vaporising the cold dampness of the mist condensate. She gasps at the festering hot air. The room is entirely saturated with a dank and clammy darkness. The tiny pores of the cement walls seep, in places the heated fluids trickle down in flowing acrid streams. Her cloths become greased with sweat. Slowly the pupils of her eyes adjust to the darkness, adding visibility back onto her list of senses. In the rear of the room a pack of dogs amass in one corner, resting and collapsed herd-like against each other. Piled up and slumped on the concrete floor, some occasionally shuffle and fidget amongst the pile, their bellies filling with air and slowly deflating, while others fester, their bodies stiff and unmoving, their mangy hides punctuated with crass excrescences and scoured out indentations. In the middle of the cement floored room is a large ash heap. One of the larger dogs flickers into movement, its huge body moving in the darkness at the rear, its jaws grapple around the thin bony ankle of one of the deadens. It lurches and heaves the carcass out of the pile, at once releasing a stench of wet

11

damp pestiferous fur, almost enough to make the girl lurch forward the contents of her own stomach. The girl watches patiently as the larger dog drags the carcass, yanking it across the cement floor, clutching the sinewy ankle in its mouth. A smeared mucilaginous trail is smeared out across the floor marking the path where the dog was dragged. The girl's eyes gleam, transfixed by the swaying, buoyant movement of the dog's genitals, as it braces its stocky legs, dragging the carcass with jabbing successive heaves. The dog rests the carcass in the center of the ash pile. With her hand clasped over her nose and mouth, the girl splashes the petrol from a metallic can, onto the carcass of the dog. The larger dog looks on, seemingly indicating the timing of the event. The girl reaches forward and lights up the carcass, at once it becomes engulfed in flame, the light splashing against the walls of the room, flames are soon licking up to the cement ceiling. The room too fills with copious amounts of grey smoke that funnels out the opening onto the balcony and sways dizzily, as it collides against the cool cold air outside. The girl emerges onto the balcony immersed and somewhat carried by the torrent of smoke emerging from the room.

The cremation is short lived and not too much later the pile is once again an ash heap of smouldering entrails. In a sparsely lit corner, the girl and the dog routinely pass their time indulging in different children's games. Like a deranged child, the girl sits over a jigsaw puzzle, hammering two individual pieces of the jigsaw together, deliberately forcing the non-connecting pieces into conjugation. Her face snarls as she pushes and beats the individual pieces, forcing their curved ridges into alignment, sometimes no matter how resistant they are. Gleefully she interlocks the jigsaw pieces in haphazard conjunctions, which fragment and disassemble the final image, producing random juxtapositions and disjointed intersections of colour and motif. The outcome is a micro-collage, engendering not a completed representational or even objective image, as what is normally anticipated, but a fragmented and jagged edged surface of buckled and bent up fragments, arranged in almost random conjunctions. Pieces of sky, of face, of walls, curtains, tables.. all become disaggregated and strewn higgledy-piggledy over the entire surface. Nor is a quadrilateral shape produced, where the overall size is pre-determined by the border pieces, but instead something that is no longer delimited by a border, eliciting an evolving and irregularly shaped perimeter. When all the pieces of the puzzle are affixed in a place the puzzle is determined as completed. At the end of each completion she reads aloud a phrase from a book. She then rips out that page and feeds it to the dog. She then breaks the puzzle back into its individual constituents to again repeat the task. Each time the pieces are connected in increasingly different ways, always producing a different outcome. With each succession the individual pieces become increasingly more malleable. The child is bewildered by this concept, she repeats the task until the jigsaw edges have become sufficiently pulverised that ultimately any two selected pieces can be conjugated together, thus allowing a near infinite variation in the final output.

But her real objective lies elsewhere. With its bloated eyes squinting the dog excretes out from its arse, what appears to be a page onto the floor. At once the girl snatches up the page. She recognizes it as one of the pages from the book that she had fed the dog, only the words have been rearranged, crapped out and skew-whiffed. She reads the text aloud:

rub motion - wind sickness burning - wave darkness burgeoning in sockets - silent and shaking - she sparks - word listening - gleaming sweat vomit shaking - hand shoved between fracture - simultaneous vomiting and orgasm - wipe it on the Spanish curtains - shoes and overcoat wet through with congested dream - wracked out to mutated last dawn - breath of singed ghost - like lick of diarrhoea sweat - silver junction illuminated in film debris - sound of horses urinating - blurred street scene of forgotten traffic - numbing abandon still reeling - gush of wind flesh wafting through subways - faint tightly patched squares - static crashing against the wall, falling down giddy - vibrating rust contour - tattoo sinking between flesh in rhythm refrain - a shrug of cold merciless sorrow - vanishing into battered tank field.

She smiles to herself, hastily folding the page and placing it aside with some others. She again recommences activity on the puzzle. Her white hands flicker in the murky light as she works, tirelessly selecting, arranging and placing the pieces. The dog, having seemingly grown disinterested in the game, outstretches its wet paw into the jumbled and misformed conglomeration of interlocking pieces. The movement pushes and upturns the pieces, dislodging and tearing a hole in the surface of interconnecting bits, that was steadily forming in front of the girl. She cries out against the intrusion. The dog nudges again with its paw, dislodging still more of the pieces of the puzzle. The dog gestures towards a scrabble board, the letter tiles strewn about its surface from a previous, but uncompleted game. The girl sneers, but willingly complies with the dog's suggestion. The girl and dog adjust their positions, so that each are sitting at opposite ends of the playing board. The girl repositions a few of the letter tiles, and tediously wipes the accumulated deposits of ash from the playing board. Both then arrange and peruse their letter tiles. The dog is the first to add a word to the game board and the girl quickly reciprocates. The playing progresses and the board becomes filled with cris-crossing words. Intermittently they argue, gesturing their objections, as to whether some words are in the dictionary or not. "Burroughs says we gotta, "rub out the word," but I reckon it much better to eat out the word," says the girl, "and shit out the word, that too is good." Her spoken words seemingly burst up the silence, scattering

13

and tearing it open in all directions. The words seemingly circle without eliciting any immediate effect, as though there were some insurmountable distance between her and the dog, through which the words had to traverse. But she was certain that she could almost sense the thought slowly cranking amidst the incongruous, narrow apertures within the dogs mangy brain. Interest resumes in the game as the girl closes in on the dog's lead, grinning as she places her new word onto the board. The dog looks on, sucking one of the little plastic letter tiles, repeatedly rolling it with his tongue, as he figures out how to maintain his lead. Using his huge canine teeth the dog suddenly crunches the little plastic tile, chewing it, he grinds it up into an easily digestible substance. The dog swallows it down. With the side of its head brushing against the floor, it manages to bite onto a second tile. The girl wide eyed looks on aghast as she speculates at the concept for a while before, picking up one of the little plastic tiles with her small grotty fingers, she delicately places it into her mouth. She grips the tile holding it pressed between her teeth. Pressing lightly the small tile fractures. She is surprised, she pulls out the broken off fragment, gawks at it momentarily, glances towards the dog, and again places it between her teeth. The folds of skin around her eyes bunch together as the tile fractures a second time, cracking with the sound of a child biting into the hardest of candies. She moves her tongue, licking and sliding over the tiles brittle fractured edges. With her molars she grinds the white fragments into a pulpy white substance. She swallows and immediately picks up another. She crunches and chews up the second tile pulverising it into a white stony gravel. She swallows that up too. They are soon gulping down the letters one after another, some almost whole. The girl unceasingly snatches them up off the playing board and stuffs them into her mouth. She eyes momentarily the dog who is closely following step, but the dog is finding it somewhat more difficult to get the letters into its mouth. Now a gutty sweaty vomit fills the girls aching stomach, the contents swell and heave against the bulging stomach walls. As the letters swirl and clump together, they become tangled and form words in her stomach. With a sudden muscular upheaval her stomach walls squish together and the contents of her stomach puke out all over the floor, forming sentences and stammered utterances. The dog lurches back, spilling the contents of its mouth. The girl glances over the gluggy contents of her stomach, splattered out over the concrete floor like a book ripped up and thrown in the wind. She reads with her finger:

swallowed scream - vanishing in corrugation anomaly - word burning - sound of voice mutter left in empty drawer - metal moaning, chasing bird - someone shuffling up a hallway several streets away - the hum of amplified cellular explosions - drunk in wardrobe heap - like lick of blood sweat - mud dried on cement edge - flesh grabs in singed folds of symmetry - bent up in corridor sleep - shimmering reflection in basin water - shuddering in ghost like solitude spasms - a vomited river of screaming skulls - ejaculated paint splatters - my tongue burnt to ashes - clumped, frantic dislocation - a slurry of stiff necked moments - cold finger probing through blood-wet cavity - ghost urine found in leaking passage - conjugation delirium burgeoning - word moaning in rummage debris - word machine don't need no shock absorbers.

Suddenly its the dogs turn, as a torrent of puke surges out from between its jaws and splashes down in the spot where the girl had puked. The girl now attempts to re-read the passage:

swallowed scream - vanishing in corrugation anomaly - word burning - sound of voice mutter lkflqal ikdl ipoe.md lskk kdlakd aning, chasing bird - someone shuffling kllkd iqlskcikjld kdl ios.e kiolsnid kdiusl hum of amplified cellular explosion fkdihhkslldi isolidjs lsjf slijdeu tkjdhl k blood sweat - mud dried on cement vtrdklsj dkljlai jhcvkdwolkkdk s folds of symmetry - bent up in klsakl kdil ewerisl dkilskks la jklspi lkd in basin water - shuddering in ghost halkdi koslke kso werrr slis vomited river of screaming skulls - ejaculated tysllkd lskl kls kls qleks col to ashes - clumped, frantic dislocation – ughsl kilakd wislwwla uglsik alks gor- cold finger probing through blood-wet tusiol dklwek alddil bicxin leaking passage - conjugation delirium burgeon hioj,dmi qildvnsk ck in rummage debris - word machine don't need no shock absorbers.

She shakes her head disappointingly, the skin on her forehead twitching into a cross frown. She wipes her mouth with the back of her hand. Her limbs and posture slump inwards, collapsing as though into a boneless mass of flesh and bodily fluids. The dog gets up, its huge unwieldy body swaying like a drunken puppet elephant, dizzy from the purgations. The dog moves around the perimeter of the room, flickering through the faint light patterns shining in through the sliding door, finally merging into the darkness at the rear of the room. His sinewy muscles tighten into stiff clumps of taut leathery flesh as the darkness crawls and meanders over his body, the fetid heaviness smothering and sliding wavelike against his body. The dog emerges from the light dragging one of the dog carcasses. The leather collar around the neck of the carcass is held in the salivating jaws of the dog, the collar jerks back and forth, taut then slack, as the dog heaves the body along the ground. The dog hauls the carcass onto the ash heap at the center of the room. The small girl is already holding the petrol can in readiness, grinning and nodding to the dog. The dog steps away from the ash heap, at once the girl moves forward and pours petrol over the dog carcass. The viscous fluid splashes down over the hide of the dog, spilling into its wounds, and trickling and pouring over its back and belly. The girl stands back as the carcass erupts into vociferous flames and splashes of smoke. She runs out onto the balcony as her intestines begin to boil with the intense heat.

15

She falls panting against the railing, her reeling head dangling over the rail, her eyes spinning, staring downwards at the concrete surface so many floors below. At once the icy air permeates into her porous spindly body. The sudden temperature change is almost enough to make her black out. Snot fills her nose. Slumped over the railing she swallows at the cold air with barely the energy to move her jaw and lungs. She feels the flow of scorched air surging out from the little doorway behind her, the torrent bellowing past her, surging up into the frozen sky above. It surges and impacts, ricocheting and blasting against the cold air mass. Pieces of ash spin off into the air and float down languidly twirling as they fall down to the ground. She wipes the ash muck from her face, pushing it up into her grey cindery hair, leaving her face somewhat streaked by her hand. She remains outside until she regains her composure. She looks back and forth across the sky for the little black bird, but she cannot catch sight of it. The surges of smoke soon dwindle into wisps of rippling heat haze. The coldness once again penetrates into her body. She turns and goes back inside. Inside the dog is standing near the center of the room. Around the dog a chaotic assemblage of jigsaw pieces, scrabble letter tiles and playing cards swirl and twirl in tangled warped gyrations, that merge and separate amidst the circling smoke wisps. The entire room was quite literally brimming with whirring shreds and torn off fragments that twirled and circled in and out of tight little eddies. Smaller particles were tearing off larger ones, forming their own trajectories until the entire room become a seething mass of swirling fragments. Everything blurred into a heated micro-collage of static.

LIQUID CONVULSIVE

Liquid air attaining a somewhat viscous, cold stagnation permeates into my dry withered flesh. Inside my head the cement floor is perfused by small puddles of reflecting water, greyish sweat, blood and trash. A low cement ceiling with piercing lights forms parallel lines which converge into a distance of smoke and giddy haze. Frayed electrical cords dangle obtrusively from the pulpy white ceiling. The sound of water dripping and seeping incessantly. Sections of my head remain collapsed and impenetrable. It is dying, withdrawn and estranged, like a cement construction strangled by some colossal beast, squeezed in the huge muscular hand of god. Bruised metal bones project through the concrete slabs like fractures that cannot surrender, that cannot exhume tears of blood, the incapacity to express pain, to cry out, to respond to any kind of torture.

Debauched and lustful, a sublime indulgence, a scavenge without reward, a crying senseless bewilderment. The infrastructure creaks in deep indefinable tones, micro-fractures, evocative and without reason. Cracks appear in the walls of my head like licked out wounds. An eerie continuum of sound becomes apparent, a muttering drowsy laxative, a delinquent French dialect. A billboard in a foreign language depicts the face of a young dark-brown haired woman, white skin, freckles and curvaceous lips. A smooth lipstick of red scribbled graffiti creates a voluptuous image the advertisers had missed, leaving a shy distracted and introspective images, sullen and dirty at the same time. From all directions brown and lime green, liquid surreal fragments intoxicate and dissect my vision. The walls are coated with lime-green ceramic tiles, exo-organs, liquescent and somehow appearing penetrable. The tiles of my body are cracked and when missing expose grey squares forming images which allure and scratch the peripheral edges, the far out domains of a wounded consciousness. On several occasions my body is beset by nauseating quakes, the whole building becomes consumed by vibrations and asphyxiations.

An indefinable hunger had reached my stomach by now, one totally unsatisfiable, not a result of a desired quantity but with respect to a specific taste, texture and smell. The evident smell was however not with respect to my internal, intestinal desires, but external - and specifically that of pool chlorine, capturing childhood flashbacks, recollections of indoor pools and echoing sounds of arms splashing through the water surface. Swimming to the deepest section of the pool and testing the duration you could maintain yourself without an oxygen source.

I felt wet hands embrace me but it was not true, the warmth was comforting though. I burst onto the water surface as awakening from a heavy searing dream. With barely the energy required I gripped the lime-green tiles, feeling my body becoming limp and unresponding. The female in the billboard seemingly griped me under the armpits and lifted me to the surface. Her face, her hair falling, her smile evanescing, gone chasing into a deep rustic void. The damp shoulder I had suddenly felt, was now gliding into imperceptibility. Truth is deception, begone with such tiny circles.

A soul ferments in silence, burning ashes in scorched air. It's words spat on the ground, trodden on, refused and banished. A ceiling covered in blackened mad scribbles, scoured and torn open, painted with a knife. Scratching the walls in vacant darkness. Thermal wound ejaculation.

Grey birds hovered in the crumbling pulpy sky, circling, looping and twirling. Their grey voracious squawks echoed, flying off into imperceptible dimensions and makeshift spatial clatter. Their grey somber shadows glistened and drifted over the emptying city. The pack diverged and reformed in a continuous voracious flux. Their wings streaked through the air, spiraling, fluttering and glistening. Their faces swept grey with wind.

I stood below on the beaten earth, amidst piles of dusty old books, pages strewn out and cracking torn cement. In my small puerile hand I held a small handful of wilted flowers, lilies tied up with string, in my other hand, I held a heavy can of paint.

The attack against writing is an attack against instruments attaching viral excrescences to the body. Burroughs put it simple - the word virus must be counted with the cut-up. The process of psychic-inscription is that which attaches all the utterances of mamma-papa, god, capital, career, race and power to the body. The process of psychic-inscription, the word being its most useful viral agent, is that which devitalises the body without organs, burdens it with it's own vanity and oneselfness, trammeling it of all its multifariousness, maliciously disfiguring the thousand folds of the organism. The cut-body counters the uselessness of vanity, the mono-dimensionality of the self, the obvious vainness in actually being somebody.

In a sniffling and whirling splatter I excreted a vomit of words. I probed the wound on my shin where a savage dog had bitten me only yesterday. At first I circled my fingers around the wound, pressing on its craggy sides, then I moved my fingers into the indented and mucky surface within, tracing out the indentations of where the dogs teeth had torn through my flesh. I picked at the dry scabby surface. The image of the wild mangy dog bounding away with the morsel of flesh in its mouth still held fast in my fragmented fleeing thoughts. I wiped my bloodied fingers on the cement surface. Taking off the lid of the paint can I slopped the bristles of the brush into the shiny blue liquid. I twirled it around in the can a moment, before slopping the brush over the bite wound on my leg. Now blue immaculate, the wound was at least no longer pussing red, it stung a little, but the splash of bluishness made it altogether bewildering. The surrealists had always understood the colour blue as evoking the subconscious, as somehow connected with the unending vacuous expanse of sky and ocean.

"It's time, It's high time!," I heard.

I am a body that has no need of organs. I have no need of "I". And have declared a war against the fouled up organs of oedipus, that trap and bind the subconscious, occluding the flood of chaotic intense transformations, trammeling all the formations of distended inter-reality. I have gutted myself of all memory, torn out identity and sexuality, to be an orphan amidst a thousand molecular sexualities, a thousand mutant DNAs. I am all the shit of Artaud. Hours of abandonment, a fugitive amidst fast flutterings, chasing pages, shimmering disequilibriums, bursting strata and unbounded existential fluxes. "Louise, dans la mouise" (étre dans la mouise, to be in a mess, depressed state). Here where corporeality flickers, where a plane of machinic-desire folds out against the surface of the earth. I am a heated collage of explosive gravel, an eye caught between the teeth of Artaud. Alone, having drifted out too far, wandered abandoned, having fled into the paradoxical solitude of non-solitude, the crowding herds of solitude, a solitude so full to bursting, of jittering and hysterical laughter and stammering chattering, whispering voices. The intense fervour and joy of verging, of fleeing towards the oblivion, yet always escaping oblivion, always tricking it, always pulling out just in time, always finding another offshoot, always folding back, always laughing - because there is always something better than death. To be stuttering and teetering at the edge, at the threshold, but never so close as to plummet, because desire always finds something better than oblivion - there is always something more than death!

- Which self?
- No, the shelf!

I stood up, dusting the grey ash from my hair and shoulders. Surrounding the vicinity are seemingly monstrous blocks of white concrete, mirrored building walls and construction rubble, spread densely with layers of heaped and scattered papers, foreign dictionaries, shredded books, socialist newspapers, diaries and art magazine photocopies, their pages fluttering and twirling chaotically in the wind. I dipped my brush into the paint can. Again and again, splattering and flecking the paint in arcs, I smeared the entire space with blue speckles. The entire vicinity became splattered and splashed with drips of flecked paint. Shaking-and-pouring, squirting and spraying it, I flecked the entire expanse with blue splatters, saturating blue scintillations, sky over everything. Floating point error.

PLASTICINE

"To love someone you've got to hate your Self," her voice resounded, dominating the underlying silence. She is on the patio, sipping Pepsi and eating strawberries in the warm sun. She grins knowingly, decidedly joyful, her eyes adrift in the white shimmering sky. Her face is flushed, she breathes slumberously. In the distance is the rumbling sound of a themepark rollercoaster clattering and creaking on its metal tracks. It's metal frame gleams radiantly in the intense heat, like a giant musical construction it's sounds wail and reverberate across the distance.

Her lips fold and crumple, "What is a girl alone?," she asks. "I mean is it possible? Can one ultimately be genuinely alone?" Her forehead twitches into neat little folds of skin. " For, when one is conventionally alone, one is really only alone with their thoughts, their body and so forth. Yet the closer one comes to being entirely alone, the more one realizes the multitude. The closer one is to inanity the closer one is to infinity." She smiles, but she is still not sure. "What can a girl alone be?" she wonders. She sees herself at the end of a long darkly lit hallway. No rooms enter into this hallway, so it is really a cul-de-sac. A twirling flux of leaves blows around her and spreads loosely over the ground. The damp leaves feel cold beneath her bare feet. She is walking towards the end, feeling the cold air penetrate deeper into her pores. Briefly she turns her head behind to see if the entrance is still there. The small frame of light shines meekly out. She continues on, seeking her answer. "Must there always be only one end," she figures, "And how strange it is to find a cold wind here." Soon it is no longer leaves that are fluttering around her, but shreds of torn pages. She is fascinated by her observation that the hallway has become wider. Then she ponders, perhaps she has only become smaller. She thinks again of herself in the sun on the patio, trying to recapture the sun's warmth shimmering on her skin. The thought holds momentarily but cannot sustain itself to the extent it had previously, it abruptly slips from view, evanescing into the distance. From the sun to the shade there is always a sharp contrast, in the shade bodies are stiff and brittle, they fall apart easily. She is overwhelmed by the diffractive movement of her limbs, a whole mechanism of machines whirring and gyrating, a whole flux of turbulent gestural spasms, flows wavering and shivering, machines pulsating and grinding. The entire contraption seemingly bustling and quaking. It is now shreds of torn off flesh that flutter around her, bustling in a noisy commotion. Her own she wonders? She laughs whimsically into the darkness. Her bodily fragments move dizzy in the surrounding blackness, her organs hiss and shake like eviscerated animal intestines. She is enthralled by her own sense of estrangement from anatomical structures. Her body is disassembled into a flux of rumbling vectors... Glistening and congealing, an oily vomit suffuses the road's gravely surface... A space fuzzy and blackened... A concussive transfusion plummeting from open jaws... Unbalanced shimmerings, floating and purgative.

She reappears, fidgeting with a cigarette smeared with her own bloodied finger prints. She then stirs suddenly as if startled and braces her head upwards smiling suggestively. "We are silent together," she says, resuming her soliloquy and posture, "Numerousness gathers all silence." Her voice scrapes and grinds, hissing static and cackled laughter. Flourishing over her body are small white feathers which grow out of her skin. Small ones occasionally break off and drift whimsically in the wind. The feathers are yet too small to enable her to fly. Bemused she selectively smooths and neatens up the tousled and unkempt edges of her feathered skin, longing for that moment of magnificence when they will be strong enough to lift her frame delicately into the air. She watches the small feathers flutter and lift slightly as she glides her arms through the air. Sometimes she stands with her hair blowing in the rain, on the ledge of a girderbridge, the voice in her head screaming, "Jump, Jump..." But she won't let that come of her. With an undertoned voice she whispers, "Numerousness engenders machinic disquietude." She sniggers and the mis-en-scene fractures into an array of stray diagonals and intestine scribbles coiling and knotting.

Girl with plasticine leg bludgeons fiercely with a hammer, mashing apart her limb, shouting, "BLOOD-GEON... BLOOD-GEON... BLOOD-GEON!" She stands looking over her mangled leg and at walls splattered with grey plasticine. She hops over towards the wall, sliding the body down. Girl masturbates with fingers of plasticine, a fascination for the mingling of red oil and greying plasticine. She intones her little melody,

> I'm one of those machines that burst apart
> I'm one of those machines that reek and stink
> I'm one of those machines that scream in your ear

She smiles, her eyes are full and black, her straight black hair trails over her face, it feels damp and tangled. She resumes her roundelay, still frigging with her fingers as they whirr and gyrate (wo)manically.

> I'm one of those machines that burst out laughing
> I'm one of those machines that explode into dust
> I'm one of those machines that piss on the sky

She sings and laughs, babbling and murmuring to herself. She gasps with a shrill voice, squealing with delight as she pulls and jerks in all kinds of pirouetting motions. The mechanical movements shudder and spin as she switches the drive mechanisms. The plasticine bubbles and leaks over her fingers, spattering all over the floor in foamy red secretions. A permeation of red and grey lava erupts from her body, drenching and suffusing into a melange of feathered skin, blood and ruptured entrails. "But you've still got to hate your Self."

VIDEO GAMES

"...like stones scattered through grey grass."
"Stones can't be scattered through grass silly," replies the authoritative voice of the young girl. The first voice recommences, "...like thoughts bent up in corners, gathered in knots, incessant contorting postures." The voice breaks off when the girl smothers the younger boy's mouth with her hand. She herself continues, "You can't be a stone scattered through grass, it's simply not real! Now come on!" She grabs the boy by his small plumpish arm, and wrests him away down the corridor. Her muffled stammers depart down the corridor, echoing as they retreat.

The multilevel shopping centre carpark is again silenced. Smoke from a nearby factory streams into the floors of the carpark. The blackened mist, swells and oscillates in direction to the changing wind current. A boy hunched in a corner slides his naked buttocks along the blackened concrete floor. With a pair of scissors he cuts off his hair, cutting it into strands. He then strews the discarded clumps of hair onto the oil streaked concrete floor and smears his body through it. The rotting smell of his fish entrails spill out over the surface of his gnarled and oily-hairy skin, permeating into the damp sick air. The feverish quakes shimmer over his naked body. For some time he remains still, purged, naked and cold. His heavy hooded eyes are wet and cold, his face covered with sweat, his body bruised.

He slides his draggled and lethargic body into the grimy darkness of the corner of the carpark, partially concealing his body in silhouette. Suddenly the crisp glow from a computer screen spills out into the air, illuminating the silhouetted contours of his body. The erogenous curves of his shoulders, chin and stomach are outlined in penumbral ridges of fazed, glaring light. He sits, staring into the laptop, making adjustments. A video camera propped up on a stand also comes into view. The image on the computer screen depicts the space on the concrete floor where he had just been. He now adjusts the lens of the camera, pushing and manoeuvring the entire contraption, as he repositions it. He returns to the laptop. Hovering over the screen, he again flicks through the various menu options, dabbling about pressing the different keys. Finally a dim black and white image of himself flickers onto the screen, responding, mirror like, in real time. He looks at the grainy image for a second, before again switching and swapping through the menu options.

Waves of blackened mist beat against the flimsy exterior of the building, gushing and spewing through it's hollowed multi-levelled body. He

24

senses every movement within the building, every flutter and rumble as if the building were itself part of his body. As though the building were itself a bloated enlargement of his carcass, hollowed out and disembowelled. For a moment he is dismayed and perplexed by the simulation, he scrutinizes the bruised and battered surfaces that envelope him, in awkward frustrated glances, he becomes increasingly uncertain as to whether they are a part of his own, or that of an Other. He touches the different surfaces, fingering and caressing, in an attempt to discern between the different surfaces. He moves his fingers over wooden, concrete, steel and skin surfaces, each remaining a part of himself, and yet not at all. His body has gone astray, anonymous and unsigned. His senses are lost, double crossing and floundering amidst voids. He feels the weight of the entire structure permeating through his body, the structure collapsing within him, pulling him down, trammeling and preventing his movement. As though with every might he ever had, he could not budge the heavy cumbersomeness of his body. It's ceaseless presence becoming unnerving.

He reels around, his face taunt and bewildered. His mouth stretches agape, his eyes squish into the folds of loose blubber encircling his eyes, his lips elongate like stretched raspberry chewing gum. The metal container of an oil can, held in his hand flashes in the diffracted fuzzy light. At once, he upturns the oil can and douses the contents of the oil, spilling it over his head, shoulders and stomach. With the brushed flick of a cigarette lighter his body is a mass of yellow sputtering light, burning and incinerating. Smoke and splashes of blood bellow forth from the swelling and contorting heap.

The image of his body is seen, reciprocated in a small sub-window of the computer screen. Its grey screen image capturing the seething and contorting motions of his inflamed body.

The flames devour his body as he convulses and reels from side to side. His limbs splash through the air propelled by frantic compulsive movements. Thrusting back and forth with jerking seizures, the limbs repeatedly seize and grab sporadically in the air. The limbs oscillate in recoiling and bursting motions that force the entire body into a hurling chaotic dance.

Overwhelmed, the body now resides in a motionless condensed fractal blur. The thuddering and chugging sound of an air conditioning unit is all that pervades the audio track.

Suddenly a movement imparts flickers onto the image. And just as suddenly, the video camera topples from its upright position and crashes hard against the concrete floor. The camera totters back and forth, reeling and rolling from side to side as it searches for a new centre of gravity. The image finally regains its steadiness. From the ground an oblique image is seen of his quivering fingers and an oblong perspective of his thigh.

The glint of the blade of the scissors flickers in this jittering hand. An arm wavers above his chest. He punctures the blade into his stomach, penetrating the skin. Magnetized shimmering globules of crimson blood leak out from the incision hole and trickle down over the furrows of his rib cage. After further aggressive stabbing blows his belly is torn agape and a blackened crevice yawns open. The cold hand, loosely holding the scissors, slumps limply against the blood splattered concrete floor.

He opens his eyes and sees himself burying his stomach at the edge of a desert. His stomach, looking like a hessian bag, which is crammed full of shit and glue, lies eviscerated on the sandy ground before him. His bloodied hands penetrate into the hot sandy soil, scooping out the sand, handful after handful. Soon a small hollow crevice lies between his legs, amply large enough to bury the stomach. With both hands he holds his stomach before him and lets the slippery tangled bulk slide down through his fingers and drop into the hole. He heaps and pushes the pile of earth back into the hole. Only now does he discover that his limbs and fingers are those of a child, his own as a child. He gazes at his stumpy rounded hands, smooth and soft, but covered with a mixture of glutinous blood and speckled with gravely sand. He wipes his hand through his hair leaving a streak of sticky blood and sand smearing his brow. He stands up from his kneeling position, revealing the huge darkened crevice in his abdomen where his stomach once was. He glances up at the horizon and the sun blazing up high. The horizon fluctuates in little waves, a mirage of blazing sulfurous heat. A smile emerges between his plumpish lips, as the murmuring grate of the wind swirls around his ears. He considers his boyish physic, looking wondrously at its stunted angles, contours and dwarfishness. He pushes his hand into the gaping crevice from where his stomach was wrenched from. Straining and contorting within the pit of his belly, his arm twists and pushes in deeper. Finally the hand emerges out the other end, out of his arse. He bends his head around looking at his hand, as it jitters and wavers, responding to his commands, dangling out of his behind like an misplaced appendage. With a gruff spluttering sound he yanks his arm back out. He falls over laughing with delight.

KUN(S)T

Reposed at the foot of the intersection of the floor and the wall, her naked body leaked red mucous onto the cold white floor. She did not know whether the floor was the performance space, the surface of the earth or a mere void space constructed in her head. She decided that it didn't really matter. She consisted of nakedness and nothing; no shoes, no jewellery, no lipstick, no suntan. She was just a hideously faced girl with ugly dog teeth. Her long dark hair hung loosely over her skin, that stretched over her bony shoulders. She felt the dry insides of her stomach, still filled with the sand she had been desperate enough to eat yesterday, the desert building up inside her. She swallowed, imagining to herself the image of the saliva mixing with the sand in her stomach. She wiped her greasy nose with the knuckle of her finger, at the same time sensing the dryness and aching in her throat, tongue and eyes. She sat motionless, like a doll on a little girl's shelf, but she didn't like that, in fact, she hated that, she wanted to scream, to scream eternally, to scream until she could scream not... a screaming smothering gasping.

She took hold of a portable tape-recorder and radio unit that lied beside her on the white surface of the performance space. The recording device consisted of the main unit and two compact little speakers each about 6 by 6 cm. She stretched out the metal aerial and tilting the device (in a way that the outstretched aerial, dinged against the cement floor) she switched the radio on, and proceeded to search through the different radio bands and frequencies. "Nothing but static, nothing, nothingness, nuttiness...," she stammered, pronouncing the words in her own slurred dialect. In her immediate frustration, she shook the instrument fiercely, thumping it's red plastic cover repeatedly against the ground in convulsive aggravation, scoffing out inaudible speechless gibberish. Her face contorted, swallowed up by the furrows in her brow that formed ripples over her flesh. For a few moments her movements vacillated, swaying awkwardly delirious and oscillatory. "Busted!" she scoffed. Again recomposing herself, she resumed her attempt, maxing out the volume, she again switched between the different radio frequencies, contrasting and oscillating the distorted static tonalities, the blurred fragmented speech, the fragmented dialogues. Nothing clearly audible could be found on the dial, it was entirely crammed with garbled spluttering, nothing but chaotic squealing frequencies occasionally punctuated with the blur of distant radio stations fading in and out, all in distorted abrupt stabs and waves of static. It was an inevitable alienating frustration, less the matter of a desert of sand and bareness like that within her, but more so one of a conceptual and ontological disposition, a wasteland of overcode and overabundance. She slid the machine onto the ground between her legs, feeling the exact vibration and buzz of the little amplifiers on the inside of her thighs. She placed a cassette into the machine and slapped close the little door. For a short duration she recorded the disorganized frequencies and subliminal vocalizations emitted by the radio and their strange uncoordinated conjunction and textuality. She rewound the cassette and listened to it. She pulled out the cassette and stuck it into the second door and pressed the rewind button, grabbed another blank cassette and stuck it into the first door. This time she played the first cassette, and recorded onto the second, overlaying it with her feverish droll voice stammering out the words:

> friction of breath in narrow opening
> holding the tense manic deliria
> heaped fracture in folding wound
> refracting thru narrow naked sweat
> wrist bent up in sperm bone entanglement
> anal-ogized in cluttered ruttiness/runniness
> bruised word flesh diffusion
> vomit filled wind-gap in split void
> swollen anus in the midst of clumsy spasm
> scintillometer music

> clogged vessels of string burgeoning
> ravaged, furled out in sky retching fever
> burning breaths/static stammers
> biting toys, unhinged and sprawling abused
> stumbling over backwards, falling clotting
> dishevelled mania, mouth gaping
> splattering into worn fleshy interior
> heavy stiff sudden fraying
> cavity weeping in skin void
> insect stridulation/masturbation

> ejaculation face soaking in window wind
> hair spilling in drowned silent heaving
> collapsed fragment drowsy scintillation
> tongue buried and no one always
> the rumbling, fidgeting cacophony/symphony
> distilling thru the endless stupor
> fluttery abandonment in folding rapture/rupture
> impassioned and vibrating insatiably
> schizophrenic word winding/binding

She snickered and gasped. Growling animalistically, snorting and scoffing, she listened to the sound of her muffled voice emitted from the tiny round speakers. Her huge pink camel tongue swiped along the dry outer rim of her lips and eyes. Her dark eyes shimmied in the broiling, rippling heat and molten muckiness of her face.

Reality, finally torn off it's rusted hinge. Its skin stretched out till it was transparent. Reality was stripped raw and peeled back, translucent and fluttering, standing there with its excrescences revealed - mad, shivering, raw and deliriously exposed. The wall of reality was suddenly rubble at her knees. She could see out into distances that she never seen before. She wanted desperately to rape reality. Oh! how she wanted to fuck it. Fuck, Fuck, Fuck, Fuck, Fuck... To penetrate the bruised anus of reality. To fuck the swollen fetid arse of reality. To make reality really come! Where is the ejaculate of reality? To drill a hole through this wall, so that one and all can finally see and hear the hovering realities (Luftrealitäten), unfurling organless, the whole gamut of rhizomatic assemblages, all the sudden brinks and thresholds, and not let anyone plug the damn thing up. To make love to, to caress the raw fleshy vacuousness that was obscured by the wall of reality, to feel it really grab you and seize you tight, clenched tight, impassioned with a fierce and unremitting desire. It's heavy frothy breath whispering and muttering, its mucous moistened tongue touching and licking as you penetrate each of its orifices. To puncture through the bruised skin of reality, to flay its skin back, gouge through, until it's hovering unreality floods and spills over, streaming distended with its convulsive wirrwarr/fervour[2]. The epidermis of reality finally wounded, shattered, pierced and torn through with a million tiny orifices. Reality becoming surfaceless, nothing but expanse and depth, holes inside holes, insides and outsides indistinct and blurred indiscernibly together. All the falseness and despair of reality suddenly swept aside, excised and unhinged from all sorrowfulness.

She reached forward and pulled a large map up to herself, spreading it out over her nimble legs for her to examine. She proceed to fold it's edges about, creasing them back and forth, over and back, in different ways, so that the erratic interlacement of lines on the map collided up against different non-adjoining geographical spaces. She stared curiously at the names on the map, wondering where these places were, were they even real? She sounded out the words written on the map, as cautiously as if they were a foreign language to her. One by one, with a certain childlikeness she sounded out the names of various cities and states of the United States of America. Mind you, she had no real fascination for this place, in fact she really didn't even know of it. She turned the map around, her face straining as she followed the contours of different features, her finger sliding out along the contours of borders and highways that cris-crossed it's surface. She spun the map around again, and folded out one edge and folded in another. The spatial-temporal configuration was beset by long durations of silence, broken only by the occasional sound emitted as she folded and ruffled the ungainly dimensions of the map. She liked the way she could impinge the disparate spaces against each other, ramming them together in a collage sort of way. Randomly choosing different lines and contours, she followed along them, cutting with a pair of scissors. Soon she had numerous geographical territories all cut out and laid out separately in front of her. Then, taking the cassette tape, she pulled the magnetic tape out and began to cut that up into short sections. She then associated different pieces of the cut-up tape with the cut-out sections of the map, finally allocating to each geographical territory a short section of tape. She called it, "dada-intestines". Disgruntled she pushed the remnants of the map and tape aside. It folded and crushed itself into a heap in the corner.

Her organs hovered (Luftorgane), tangled and disgorged from her body, floating in the air like spewed out unwanted exploded electrical debris. Her sentences stumble over each other, suddenly bifurcating in different directions and voices, crumpling like bags of flesh, chocolate and wooden bones, seething like a squall of words snatched from random pages, the vomitory efflux of eaten dictionaries. Her thoughts folded and coalesced in random patterns. She squished her forehead between her hands, while constantly rubbing and wiping her face and eyes with a manic temperament. The desert within her stomach murmured and heaved, hissing and spitting. The desert within her suddenly took flight. Jolting her body as it mounted up her throat, it erupted from her mouth in a streaming spasm of sand and red dust that flung and hurtled through the air like a bursting valve. A splatter of gritty moist sand flecked all things. Some edges of the map were slightly wet. Her nose and throat were full of sand.

Grasping her hands around the edge of the microphone, she was suddenly struck by a bewildering disconcerting efflux emerging almost from outside any thought. Sucking her breath in, she delicately spread her legs apart and inserted the small microphone between her kunt lips. Feeling it's tightness her eyes filled and whirred with an ardent sense of intensification, a lethargic melting exhilaration. Her dirty bruised fingers twisted the dial to increase the volume. The sound of her kunt flowed out from the speakers, soft and beating mesmeric, her senses were overcome by the strange scatterbrain effusions buried within the fluxes of sound. She heaved and sighed, at the sound of her vaginal riff/rift. Her tongue swam amidst the blood and sand filling her mouth, her body became inundated with a fluctuating rebellious joy that drenched and suffused her limp corpo(un)reality. The oozing, gurgling sounds effusing from her kunt, were something totally bewildering to her. Her face was creased with a dizzying smile, her lips just parted and her tongue pressed against the smooth pink roof of her mouth, her breath full of the

30

sweat pulsated. With sudden unstoppable desires, she began jerking and thrusting the microphone back and forth, in and out of her kunt, frigging herself relentlessly. The sound from the speakers reciprocated, her body too, spasmodic amplified orgasms shrieked and bellowed from the small throbbing speakers. Immediately she began recording the sounds onto tape, not wanting to miss even the tiniest second. Again she thrusted the microphone repeatedly in and out of her kunt, feeling the intense rhythmic sound waves pound and splutter through the air and over her body. She was immediately overwhelmed by the way that different postures could produce different masturbatory tonalities and different rhythms as well. How different movements and positions of her legs and hips could yield strange garbled screeches and droning whining oscillations. She vacillated between different positions and different rates of masturbatory rubbing, hastily searching for the planar limits of this vaginal musicality. The sonic orgasm, with all its heady pulsation, (slow/fast, rhythmical/random, silence/cacophony) and sonic textuality (grinding, screeching, wavering, squishing, hovering and intensifying), where was this to lead her, to the most perfect conjunction of music and sex, to her genitals becoming a musical instrument, to an unlimited vastness that would fold her within her, to all musical limits becoming again unknown and pushed clear out of sight? And yet, she was yet to discover how even these tonalities would vary throughout her own menstrual cycle. Catching her breath, like she was trying to bite the air, she once again delved in, frigging herself with the microphone, at first slow, but then with increasing menacing ferocity. She frigged the microphone in and out, this way/that, until the little amplifiers were again whirring and roaring in cacophonic delirium and ear racking feedback. The static and buzz of the vibrating cones of the amplifier, the intense sonorous roar of their sonic orgasm was enough to saturate and debone her limbs in a heaving catharsis. She sighed, her body limp, gasping out in short craving splattered breaths, her whole body like a bag of wet soggy clay amalgamated with stinky molten lava, expurgated of all energy, almost demented by the boundless ecstasy of her orgasms. Her body flickered with a vibrato effect. Her kunt was speaking, it's voice was enunciating, it was there. Her kunt became a mouth, a voice, a singing genital, a vagina dentate. A kunt that mutters and stutters, like a Burroughs' asshole that talks, but instead this is a kunt hole that sings. Would this crack in reality, this hole into an existential void begin to swallow her up? Eat her up, and then spew her insides out? The vaginal (a)tonality of it all, had effused her with an utter lust that compelled her, an outlandish desire for unfettered rebellion. With the last shred of energy, she lurched forward, feeling the coldness of her shoulder slide against the warmth of her cheek, she clicked the stop button on the tape recorder, her body then collapsed and crumpled over like a floppy mannequin, drenched in reverberations of somniloquous sleep.

31

"The silence of you, the reader, your silence is like murder to me. And what could ever have been wrong with my unfettered flow of libidinal desire? And yet, were they even our's, that is as a cohesive whole, and not those of many others as well, for we have already become many. It is no longer a simple matter of your voice muttering these words in your head, but more so, one crowd impinging on another crowd, one crowd muttering to another, a total ruckus, for we are both crowds, I am a crowd, you are a crowd. These flows are more dynamic, different tangents keep butting in and flying off like sparks, all things keep getting pulled in different incongruous directions. To begin with, we can distinguish at least two distinct flows, for your flow of reading is intrinsically different from robert's flow of writing, they only connect, overlap and intersect to varying degrees, at certain times, in certain locations, through certain personae. In any case, it is quite likely that your flows may have traversed traces and trajectories that were unreachable, even unseeable to me, with the result that you obtain a different nuance a different sensation to me. What is occurring is the conjoining of these two flows, and their ravelling around and through each other, their interpenetration and co-mingling, their playful divergence and alignment, like a thousand rivers flowing into a mad sea. robert only writes with the intention of eliciting his machinic deliria, and maybe you read to elicit another, but these deliria are by no means super-imposable, they comprise different degrees and intensities, they coagulate on different surfaces, and in different rooms, they fly off in all sorts of different directions. I am only inbetween, that is between you and robert, being neither the invention of you, nor of robert, being neither real nor areal. All of our lines of flight, our hovering thoughts (Luftdenken) slip off and spill out around us, left and scattered, here and there, in empty abandoned rooms, dusty, shabby and inconceivable. Yet, what could ever have been wrong with my deviations and experimentations, my unremittent distortions, my boundless directionlessness, my absolute loss of discretion? Did we crowd things in too much? And anyway, I say, indiscretion is good! Discretion is always such an ego-centric thing that binds us to our sense of appropriateness and to authority. For how else might we find out who we are, and who we might be, and what is there, beyond language, politics, gender, race and rationality? Why should we be made to feel bad, about what is not bad? Who in society determines what makes a good feeling and what makes a bad feeling, and installs that determinism into our heads? Why must we constrain and repress our desires, even the desire of love, in order to comply with all that giggling nonsense and puritanism of the masters? Again you interrupt and say you need some time to sort out your sexuality. But I say, to be sorting out your sexuality is still better than to have sorted it out! Like why the fuck would you ever want to have something like that sorted? Sorted into what? So that you can have some deluded sense of security and certainty, so that you can crush it all down into a minuscule little oedipal

32

lump (like some impotent minuscule dick) and then think that that's it, that that's it's fullest and most expansive extent, that that's what it means? That that's who you are? Hah! I say, leave it unstable, in flux and indeterminant, unknown from one moment to the next. So I'll go wrap these shadows around me, disappear from sight, become imperceptible, unknown and cellular, crowded among my trillions of sexes, and what do I care about the little bits of reality that everyone else keeps pacing back and forth over. Hah! Those bits are almost imperceptible themselves!"

She gathered her body up again, her organs folding inwards, coagulating together like a reverse explosion. With her amplified kunt swirling and whirring, she emerged through a narrow doorway, and found herself walking out into the street. Her body was immediately swept into the flurrying clatter of faces, clothes, café smells, passers-by and advertising gimmicks of the street. A bewildering and incomprehensible coagulation of shufflers and speedsters, of strutters, stutterers and shutters. A heaving visual cacophony of blurred facades, reflections in shop windows, dirty rubbish filled gutters, windshields glinting and sparkling, cracked walls and neon lights flickering and twitching. The whole pack of humanity, squeezing and rubbing and rumbling, seemingly crowding itself together, as though to deliberately cause it's own asphyxiating downfall.

She let the crowd determine her direction, which meant that she kept moving so that she was always in the amidst of the thickest of the crowd, being dragged carelessly along, erratically changing from crowd to crowd as they successively dissipated and regrouped, she did not care if she would soon become lost. She was drenched in the streets bustling fluxial mania, in the whole screaming and shuffling, the slamming and flashing musical cacophony of the whole thing, but she was at the same time countering it too (maybe even adding to it) with of cause, her own squelching blast that emanated from her kunt. Her kunt chattering obscenities to boys on the street. The intense whirl and coalesce of her kunt blurted out, buzzing and scandalising, emerging between the other sounds, with the caterwaul of silence, muffled anxious reverb and belches of stumbling static. She was ready to blast anyone who objected to her little kun(s)t-song and the amplified kunt rhythm of her walk, that she liked so very much, ready to burst out with the shrill piercing cacophony broiling inside of her kunt, and all that she had to do was to twist that volume control to make it a little louder, to elicit its vitriolic blast of intensified, eroticized sound. The continual screeching and shrieking sound of her kunt spliced in so well with the grinding and chugging machine sounds of the street; the clattering murmur of factories and construction sites, the passing rattling throng of pedestrians, the chattering wobbling sound of her own walking, creating whole new universes of mutated sound, polyvocalised sexuality and sonic vaginal machinism.

33

Notes

1   Kunst means art in German
2   Wirrwarr is chaos in German

DEFACED CELL

The black wind lashes frantically, its harsh pulverising grind hammers at a deafening intensity into our cold and bloody ears. The black hole we are in swells and churns like a huge front moving across the sky, a deathly thickening agglomeration of black restlessness. Up in the blackened charred sky, you can see the swelling blackness stretching and smothering over an ever greater and greater expanse, like a huge bruise ballooning out over the skin of the sky. The roar and stench that comes across from its epicentre, is alone enough to make you keel over choking in madness. The wind circles around in sheets and waves, bursting and cracking against your ears, swearing and threatening to pulling out your ear drums and chew them up before your open eyes. I struggle ineptly to stand against its swirling cyclonic velocity. It wrenches fiercely, continually lurching in distraught directions as though some colossal being is displacing the air, filling it with a cold sebaceous stream of black fluid. Like someone taking an impressionist print and painting it over with thick black brush strokes, those crystal blues vanishing with each brush stroke. Everything is becoming drenched in a black mire that infuses and chokes everything in sight. It is pulling me under, spinning and swirling me like a gigantic reverse-centrifuge, sucking and constringing everything into its congested grimy core. The concussive force of the black hole suppresses all other forces of motion, all the flows are now directed towards this new centre.

All memory goes hurtling into the epicentre of the black hole, pulled there, as though black holes like eating that most of all, consequently your memory keeps pulling you back into the black hole, crushing you down - reminding you, just who you are and what you are. Memories stream over us, pouring like black sodden fogs, trudging over our bodies, glutted with blackened memory, other peoples memories, our own memories, uncertain memories. The memory fogs spiral and swirl, bursting out of our heads and accelerating stretching elongated out into the blackness. The multitude of memories mutating into only one memory, coiling around itself, always accessed, made always inseparable from the misery of the black hole. This "one memory" is what we call history and knowledge.

All our faces emerge from black holes, and all our faces project back onto, fit neatly over the face at the centre of the black hole. So that all faces become the one face, and consequently your face is in the black hole, and keeps pulling you back into it. Our faces should be alien to us,

35

a face is something monstrous and inhuman, a blurry and blubbery disfigurement staring back at us from a mirror, a joke mask. By contrast, an unalienating face is a face that floats, a smooth anamorphic surface, a face filled with anonymity and dispossession.

Some have gladly lost their faces entirely, so that they can become unrecognizable, utterly faceless, utterly nameless. They have dismantled the face and become imperceptible and unknowable. Their memories have become intertwined and confused with those of others, they cannot say "I am..." without each time having to adopt a new name. Their memory is floating and migratory, continually fleeing, to avoid the encroach of the black hole at the centre.

I stand with my face, holding my memory, burdened by injury. My face is torn and like melted wax, it is not yet smooth. The orifices gape out, protruding through the skin like senseless pried open ruptures. The wind gushes through my head, like water does to a sinking ship. The winds harsh hoarse breath beats rhythmically, its teeth gnaw at my ear, its lips slide over my cheek, its inebriated breath soaks into my gasping flesh. Here I stand, amidst the miasma of god's shit, hollow head, humanity is nothing more than bacteria scampering over the shit.

She stands there at the axis of the scene, the sleeves of her white shirt bellowing like sails about to becoming wings. Her cuffs, loose and unbuttoned flutter buoyantly in the wild wind. Her head is round and wooden, like a head cut out of a Giorgio de Chirico painting. The blank wooden grain of her face is raw and disquieting. The emptiness of it makes me shudder. She is faceless, her face is nothing but smoothness. As she tilts her head allusively, my attention is caught by the abrupt movement of her shadow, a monstrous balloon shape of darkness that sweeps across the background. The shadow's formidable form seems to magnify even further the tense disquietude of her presence. Her head wobbles whimsically, lurking; making inane any attempt to try to comprehend her exact feelings, they being somewhere far out and unreachable, somewhere far offshore. Her head moves constantly, ceaselessly changing postures; tilting, swaying and gesturing like something that is only real while it moves, the second it stops, it no longer exists. Her cloths make an obscure juxtaposition of looseness and tightness, they seem altogether too cumbersome and illcut. The surface of her wooden head is moist. A thin film of clear liquid leaches out of it's wooden pores and trickles meekly over her body. Her entire body is moist, as though she is suffering from a delirious fever, one that makes her sweat without stopping, constantly sticky. She approaches nearer, menacingly her entire body flutters and surges, vacillating with the awkward movements of a intoxicated mechanical butterfly. I reach out to hold her hand, to steady her, to touch her. For a second I feel her soft

36

skin fill my grasping hand. Her quivering body suddenly collides against mine, her vast elongated arms stretch out and fall around me, grasping me at the shoulders and pulling me in to her. Whilst holding me there in her tight grasp I sense my body shivering against hers. Her body is apoplectic, her delicate limbs gleam white in the obfuscating light, she wears heavy boots. Her arms caress searchingly, moving over my body, examining and exploring every groove and contour. Her skin feels moist and dewy, like the cheek of a child shivering in pre-dawn air. Her cloths are wet, like those of that shivering child. She touches and fondles delicately with the locks of my straggly hair. She is oddly attentive, reacting to even the slightest flicker in my facial muscles, bemused by the movement of my eyes and the slightest fluctuation in my brow and lips. The chilling mysteriousness of this woman entrances me, and yet fills me with the deepest sorrow and anguish. An altogether distraught sense of despair and aloofness seems to cave in around my cluttered sensibilities. The wind rakes across our embracing bodies, billowing my hair out like a strange dishevelled flag. Next to her, one can sense every one of her cells purging, every cell is saturated with tears, every cell bustles with whirling turmoil, soaked with desire. Within my engorged head, a ferocious mountain of pain lurches and reels in gigantic landslides. Nothing but the howling torment of the wind fills my ears, hammering and swirling like a deafening whirlpool of tears jammed inside my head.

The solitude of our bodies in this vast space, the indeterminacy of ourselves, is a sadness of indefinite origin. Our bodies becomes cris-crossed by a frustration at our own sense of corporeality, a sense of an inability to be what fringes paradoxical possibilities, what wraps rationality into a contorted mess. Her facelessness confronts my giddy discomposure, disrupting all my senses into uncertainty and irregularity. The contagious unconfined silence that she emanates stretches out and submerges me. Her mute silence envelopes us, becoming the only thing that offers any resistance and refuge against the malignant blackness that engulfs us. My sense of reality has finally jammed, and become infused with unstable molecules. Our bodies are jammed into the immense obfuscating mechanisms of delirium and passion.

"I'm afraid of the immense depths that loom within, so many darkened corridors lead out of my aching burning head. I have so many quandaries, but I know most of all, that I simply cannot stay here, in the present. There are so many paths, like black ribbons streaming out of my head, fluttering out into the wind, inviting. And I know I simply cannot stay here. I know I must flutter too. The black hole is encroaching, we mustn't... we mustn't stay long." I tentatively pause, listening to the sound of my final letters reverberating in the silence, but she makes no reply, she is mute. Only the black wind shimmers over her unmoored features.

Her freakish head is bathed in streaks of intense white light, folding in ripples. The glaring light almost floating on the surface of her head. The film track shudders and blurs for a fleeting moment. At first I only hear the sound of her heavy boots crushing the marshy undergrowth, the sound, as they slosh into the dense and tangled bog of long grass and roots beneath our feet. Then her body comes into perspective, moving off in the direction towards the forest, her huge wooden head encumbering her stride. I follow after her as she makes her way up the small embankment. In the distance, the forest that emerges is black and burnt. Charr black branches tangle and contort silently against the ominous grey smeared sky. With a broken slow stammering, I struggle to keep up with the hurly-burly pace, her flickering ghostly body makes as she traverses up the embankment. Beyond the sound of our footsteps, is nothing but the silence of the wind's eerie mood. Even as we ingress into the forest not the slightest rustling movement emerges from within the guttered black forest. It is drenched in darkness. The stench of burnt wood and smoke becomes all the more pervasive as we progress. Ashes and tiny smouldering cinders bustle and float amidst the shimmering fluid air. Small embers glitter and sparkle in the thick blackened milieu. Her body almost dissolves into the charred and tangled melange. Her limbs fold into the tree branches as though the branches were part of her very own flesh. A damp heat radiates out, snapping and cracking in the otherwise silence. I wipe the sweat from my gushing wet face, smearing ash in a black smudge across my face. She pauses and sits herself in the forest, on the ashy forest floor, her back resting against the blackened trunk of a tree. If only she had blond hair I thought, what an image it would make draped out across the burnt wood? She sits in no particular spot, in just far enough that one senses ones immersion and absorption in the forest, just so far that the space encompasses you, where the light that might shine through the trees can no longer penetrate. She sits with her knees bent upright. I approach her, bending aside the embrangled and knotted twigs. She seems unsure of how to respond, stagnant and immobile. I sit close.

Next to her, her body touches mine, tense and warm. Her body is turbulent and unruly. A sharp sensation of nausea runs through my body, one which penetrates every cavity, as I feel her large wooden head lightly against mine. My body shudders with delight at the drenching shivering illicitness. Her hand reaches out and touches my face, as a child does. Suddenly the buttons on my shirt are unloosened, and her smooth ashy hand vanishes inside. For a moment I feel nothing, but then it comes, fidgeting and squirming inside. Before I can take a breath, her hand has squeezed under my bra, and caresses over my hard eager nipple. I feel my entire body lunge and roll in spasms of delirious delight, my body falling weak-kneed into her grasp. My body streams out like ribbons, a sensation of dampness floods over my limbs, my skin surges

38

with scarlet flashes, and heated gasps. I feel the flesh of my face caressing lightly against the smooth wooden bulk of her head. My skin touches against the traces of blood and ash, which lightly smear the left surface of her bulbous wooden head. Her head feels cold and clammy. I reach with my hand and touch at the back of her head. I let my fingers tips slide down the concave wooden surface, down to where her spine connects with her head. I pull my hair aside and listen with my ear to the insides of her head. Inside, her head emits a droll grinding mechanical noise, that repeatedly clanks and whirrs like a demented instrument unable to cease its burling wheeling motion. A hollow wounded sound, having the rumbling texture of a heavy wheel rolling around in a stone circular corridor. The sound of her blood pulsing and circulating resonates beneath the whirr of clattering and gyrating.

Her other hand is wooden. I stare at it residing there, on my knee. I invite it to the space between my legs. Her dry wooden fingertips glide over the smooth skin of my thighs, tenderly and voyeurously sliding up the insides. My body glistens and trembles with streaming convulsive light, my whole body contracts and expands with each breath. Her wooden fingers plummet into that space between, sinking into my soaking warm flesh, saturating and imbuing my body with torrents of nympholepsy (desire for the unobtainable). Her wooden hand creaks and swells, her fingers swirl and squirm, drilling my clit. The wooden joints slide into my vulva, vibrating and heaving in and out, in mad lascivious rhythms. The smooth wooden texture continually rubbing and thudding against my pulsating clitoris. I gasp out in delight, my body collapsing into feverous swirling seizures and desires. My clitoris bursts and screams, engulfed by hurtling pulsating machinic orgasms.

Her armpits are burning, the flames flicker out of the concave of her armpits. Her face is burning. I wrap my arms around her body, holding tight, yet I cannot at all sense the fire's heat. A stream of lava spills and exudes from her body, pooling and splattering out in vibrant rivulets. Its redness swells and glistens, inflaming and fulminating in shrieks and purgations. Her whole body breaks open, tears open, erupting and bursting into sparkling flames. Her body pours over mine, spewing out like a fiery melange of pulp. Her body wrests open, crumbling with shatterable flesh. The red muck spills and splashes out, smearing and falling over my face and limbs. The flames engulf me, I grasp her body even tighter, not wanting to let go. I become embroiled with her body, immersed in it, cumbersome and wooden. I watch as her body evanesces and disintegrates, as it sinks between the opaque shadows, leaks into the dead tree limbs and buries itself in the ground of ash and fire. Her body is almost not there, unseeable, and yet I can distinctly feel and touch her, it is because I am going with her. I am leaving with her, merging with her. I know I must flutter too. I leave her – undenuded.

UNMANNED

Huge oversized trees tower skyward enveloping the park within itself. The grey sky enigmatically acts as a giant mirror, reflecting a blurred outline of the landform below. Straining my neck upwards, I can see myself as a tiny blue speckle in the centre of the sky. In a less than explicit sense, I can in fact see where I'm going. With my head arched upwards I continue moving along the path.

The treetops fringe my peripheral vision. High up, their huge green branches rustle ominously with the heaving wind gusts. There is a sense of increasing coldness and an emerging change in the weather. A dark gloom diffuses into the park, leaking out through the densely folded branches and suffusing into the expanse. The wind scatters the leaves around my feet, striking in sudden bursts and then recoiling, returning erratically to brush and beat languidly against my body. The winds humid, inebriated breath breathes over me, as if coming from some unseeable colossal being. The wind joyously meanders, overturning everything small and light, tugging at my loose lumpen cloths.

looking upwards into the reflecting sky I notice someone is approaching. I push my bangle tightly up my arm, and scamper into the undergrowth below the trees. The forest rustles with delight, it is wet and damp. My lungs pant, more out of trepidation than exertion. I can hear its heavy feet approach scraping in the gravel, its breathing is heavy and coarse. Even closer, one can hear its labouring muscular movements. It is not a someone, but a dog. I watch its grey sunken body pass by. Silently I emerge out from the undergrowth and stand to the rear of the dog on the path. The fur on the dogs hide is scabrous and tufty. It's bloodied intestines protrude from its anus, dangling in a festering twisting clump. I scrape my foot against the stony ground and its huge mangy head bends around alerted by the sound. I push my bangle tightly up my arm and stretch a girlie smile onto my lips. It could not manage to return similar, but I inferred it was not hostile. It stagged towards me, cautiously outstretching its snout. The dog stank profusely, an open wound was chiselled into its left shoulder, giving it a awkward stumbling motion as it approached. Its clear eyes stared longingly into my face, its immense deep black nostrils continued to scrutinize, searching across my flesh. Emanating from the dog's body was a sickly feverish heat, an ill-disposed effluvium that impressed a dizzy quake through my body. I shivered looking into its weary eyes, wondering where such a thing could come from. A cold wind swept up from behind, long strands of my hair billowed forward over my face. I hunched my arms up, tucking them defensively

40

under my chin, elbows pressed together. I took a few steps back. The dog sensed my withdrawal, it hesitated a while simply staring. It then moved oblique to the path, knelt and jerked the side of its head back and forth against the gravely path. The sinewy muscles and bones in the dog's neck protruded outwards as it did so.

Its ravaged angular form trembled before me. Dishevelled and irresolute the dog lingered no more and at once abandoned from the situation. Departing with an abrupt clumsiness, it moved without suggestion, shuffling awkwardly as it went. I stood watching its grey body shrink into the ebbing light. The space was alone again. My limbs loosened and become less rigid, the soaking air permeated into my body. I looked skywards and at my miniaturised reflection barely visible with the approaching darkness. I returned my glance to the path ahead, and because of the impending cold, decided to continue further ahead.

The silence of the space had by now wrapped fully around me, gripping me with its burgeoning delirium. She stood there, shimmering at the centre of the expanse. Her appearance seemingly fluctuating in a swirling muddle of distorted reflections and shadows. I stood at a distance, examining and observing, before approaching closer. She seemed unaware of my presence, even as I drew closer. Her irresponsiveness remained uninterrupted. When the image at last became quite lucid, I was stopped aghast. Bewildered. My mouth fell open, my lip trembled. Smoke seemingly billowed out of all of her orifices, black broiling fumes that surged and heaved in vortiginous torrents. She stood there smouldering and billowing, her voice choked with black soot, blazing black fumes spewing forth from all her gaping orifices. "A girl volcano," I first thought, "but what could that mean?". Her body was more like a huge steam engine. The sound blasted against my ears and the heat scorched the air penetrating warmth into my skin. Huge bloats of smoke rumbled over the treetops. I circled around the crazed contraption, viewing it from all sides. It seemed so utterly irreconcilable, so ill-fitting to any purpose or means. Climbing narrow metal stairs, I reached atop a platform that skirted around the perimeter. Every pipe, condenser and valve radiated an intense heat, every component vibrated, resounding its cacophony through the air. At one end huge grilled air vents sucked in the surrounding air, pulling it down into a huge furnace. While at the other end, belches of smoke swelled and smothered from a choked smoke stack. The hammering clank of its many moving components ceaselessly roared at my ears as they revolved and churned on their greasy axels. I moved around the platform, looking for the operator, but found none. For a while I stood looking outwards from the elevated position of the platform, leaning against the blackened guardrail that bordered the platform. I pondered to myself, what was this inane contraption, from where had this cantankerous mechanism come from?

By morning I awoke. The machine had come to a stop during the night and now lay silent and still, small whiffs of grey smoke drifted off from the top of the smoke stack. The sky was clear and warm. I shook off the debri of ash and soot that had accumulated in my hair and on my skin, it cascaded and shimmied down through the crystalline ghost air. I eased myself off the platform and climbed down the narrow metal stairs. I moved a short distance out from the contraption before turning around. I stood a while staring, filling and convincing my eyes with the sight of its extraordinary beauty.

WALL

Her torch beam flashes through the darkness, scattering over the dreary expanse of desert gravel. All is silent except for the sound of her approaching footsteps crunching the gravel underfoot. Irritatingly, she once again thumps the side of the plastic covering of the torch, in an effort to adjust its faltering light. The beam flickers fully again and skirts amid the invariant space. She has come quite some distance since nightfall, but is now on the verge of collapsing from exhaustion. Her enervated limbs sway and wobble languidly. Her limbs are of limp and anonymous flesh. It is she herself who must bring the dawn, as it will not merely come at that certain time it most usually does. For sure, it was already well past that time. Since nightfall when she had set off, she had been without rest, scurrying across this arid terrain of depravity and blackness. Despairingly she wiped her straining eyes, and made an effort to cheer herself up. For it was beginning to seem that gravel and darkness were all that resided here, and that her exertions had been made in vain, wholly in error. Her haggard complexion was to brighten when at last something appeared at the limit of her torch beam. But as yet she could not say for sure what it was. When she finally reached what it was, she placed her hand on its surface, feeling the small cracks that extended over its massive surface. It was an old derelict wall, too high to really climb, that stretched outwards on both sides beyond the limit of the torch beam. Made out of cement, it was seemingly positioned at the very discontinuation of inanity, what was seemingly the very extremity of the reality she had encroached upon. Still she could not at all see what was on the other side. It occurred to her that it must simply be the border. She moved the torch up and down illuminating all of its surface. She then slumped down and resided at the bottom of the wall. She reposed there, with her back resting against the wall, she could feel the coldness of the concrete surface penetrate into her thinly clothed body. As a final precaution she flickered the torch beam back and forth across the expanse from where she had come. She then turned the flashlight off and was instantly engrossed by an unbroken darkness. Her eyelids closed soon after.

She was awoken by the smell of another woman, instinctively her finger pushed at the button of the flashlight. Her eyelids lifted up into the blur of scattered light. The woman's body cowered over her, her long wet hair obscuring her face. The girl defensively scuttled her body sideways in a rolling abrasive movement, that spun her body through the gravel. She fell to the side of the woman, the torch now out of reach, shined a beam of light illuminating her ankles. The remainder of the woman's body was

43

an obfuscating mass of blackness. The girl scraped and thrust her body, awkwardly attempting to propel herself away from the woman. The woman did not react, but at most appeared startled by the girls reaction. Close by, perhaps even behind her, the girl could hear sounds of squealed laughter. By this time the woman had picked up the torch, and was now standing over the girl's prostrate position, shinning its piercing beam directly onto her. For some reason, though unphysical, this seemingly caused the girl's every muscle to paralyse into rock. The woman said something, though at first it seemed to be in an unfamiliar tongue. The woman started again, "Who that?" followed by, "Alice, we are so glad, come, we have been expecting you, the dawn is still to come you know," she still seemed to have difficulty sounding out the words.

"I am not Alice," the girl replied sternly.

"Then who are you?"

"I hardly know, just at present, well... I have been someone before, but I don't know who I am now."

"There are many, there are many."

She was most confused by this last statement, to which she finally blurted out, "I have a sister named Alice, perhaps that is who you are referring to."

She only repeated her reply, "There are many, there are many." She shrugged her shoulders and stood up and followed the woman, remembering just now, that they were exactly how her sister had described them in her dream. The woman handed the torch back to the girl. She thumped the plastic cover again to correct the fading beam of light. At once its beam leapt forward and illuminated three bleached skinned children drying beside a bluish section of the concrete wall. She then sputtered the light over the legs of the woman beside her, reaching up to her naked buttocks. Her skin was supple and bleached white. She dared not shine the beam any higher, so the woman's face remained presently obscured in darkness. The woman had already noticed the girl's peculiar interest and responded in an almost whispered voice, "It is that we are unclad," but the girl thought she'd said "unglad." She skirted the beam of light back towards the children huddling and jittering beside the huge wall. Their bodies were amassed together, immersed in silence. The whiteness of their puerile bodies glistened between the folds of entangled limbs and eyes. A fiery complexion sputtered and gleamed over the whitish surface of their bodies. Small sporadic fires were burning in the space surrounding them. Wisps of grey smoke drifted through the beam of light, brushing against their bodies like fading ghosts. As the girl approached she became increasingly aware of the nauseous smell that was emitted from their bodies. Nearing closer to the children she found the ground was bespattered with a kind of oily black vomit. The girl was to observe how repeatedly, one of the children would get up, move a short distance away from the others, and retch an oily black substance onto the ground. The substance, once exhumed flared

44

up in flame, like volcanic earth instantly combusting on contact with oxygen.

The body of the woman beside her, was then suddenly assailed by a tumult of thrusting and scoffing paroxysms. She watched, as she saw her darkened figure lurch forward, and like the children, retch a shimmering wail of vomit onto the ground. The exhumations flicked into flames as she wiped her mouth with her fingertips. In the light she could see splashed trickles of the substance sliding down her legs. When the woman had regained her composure the girl though to ask, "Which please... which is the shortest way to get around the wall?" The lump of shadow that was the woman turned and made a facial expression that the girl could not make out in the darkness. A moment passed before the woman finally replied to her question, she began initially in her jerky foreign accent, but when she started again, she said, "One must become as small as an ant to pass through those cracks." It was then that the girl remarked, "That wall is so very narrow!"
"That it is, and an ant is also so very small."
The girl inanely tried to push her huge finger into one of the cracks in the wall. "When then will the dawn come?" the girl asked. The woman fell into a prolonged silence before she replied, "Perhaps it won't." The girl fell sunken with this reply, "Surely things must be simpler," she thought to herself, "How else could one get around this wall, and bring the dawn?" But the girl had come too far to be so easily daunted. The woman's hand stroked and fondled the girls hair, "Perhaps it is you that knows... that which is alone with you?"
"Silence is always alone with me," muttered the girl, "silence can only be alone." At least her sister had muttered something like that while asleep and dreaming. The girl and the woman had almost reached the children by the wall, when a woman on horseback interrupted the scene. She skilfully brought the immense beast to a jarring halt near the children. The woman on horseback towered above the girl and the other children, such that their necks all stretched upwards as they gawked at her. The saddlecloth and harness of her horse were elaborately adorned in the manner of an ancient warrior. The woman spoke in the foreign dialect to the children. The girl observed the woman's strange appearance, her cropped blond hair almost looked like a wig, habitually worn slightly crooked. Her huge white teeth stood out from her crimson coloured gums and tongue, the rows of her teeth were similarly misaligned. The woman then wrenched the horse around and disappeared, heading off in the direction she had come. Almost at once, the flock of children began giggling and brimming, almost taking flight and rising into the sky. Their bodies shimmied and flurried, seemingly swimming through the air. Their short limbs wavered and twirled in the air, as they dispersed, gliding off through the air. The girl and the woman were left alone. The girl spun around and shined the torch beam over the woman in an effort to finally

see her appearance. At the same time, she forced an awkward smile onto her lips. Yet even though she was shining the torch beam directly onto the woman, her upper torso remained obscured in a block of pure darkness. She began to cry as she stared at the harrowing sight. She whispered.....

I am,
clustered in corners,
piled up in cul-de-sacs,
pushed down crevices
and rammed between fissures.

I am,
jammed in the passage way,
scrunched up against the ceiling,
crunched up like rocks,
stuck between two walls.

I am,
knotting/nothing inside,
veering off the causeway,
broken off at the corners,
and licking my eye.

I am not.

DÉFÉNESTRE

4 of November 1995,

When all of the possible is exhausted, vanquished, turned into the doldrums of dust and expired, life itself must fold and elongate, the organs must become unfurled, to finally breathe on the outside, unfettered by scraggy bones and botched lungs. The body, with it's tireless, immortal itch of consciousness, must, like a tattered dress, be renewed, to rip itself open, break off and descend, it must lunge into the sky and so distend.

The 17th arrondissement, in a 3rd floor apartment, a man, hooked to an oxygen tank, like a dog, winces in bouts of suffocation. His quivering hand scuttles pages from the desk to the floor as his body cowers for air.

He runs his fingers over the window glass, feeling it's cold smoothness on the tips of his fingers. Straining, he reaches and pushes open the window, a withered squeak resounds from its hinges. That familiar gust of shivery air brushes over his unshaven face, pushing lightly against his grey hair. Bleary eyed and staggering, his wavering arm heaves his body against the window ledge. He sees the abyss below, a grey silence of cold cement. He wipes his sweating face. His arms extend into the open air, grasping and heaving, his breath rasping. His legs heave and push, floundering as his body suddenly tips. "Better to break the window and leap into the open air"[1]. A tumble ensues and a dull thud resonates. A shrill scream is smothered by a raspy suffocation, a final flicker of movement, a convulsing gesture, his mouth sags open, the coldness drags it's long shadow across.

The fall, the sound, the impact, the light, the trajectory, the gesture and final vocalisation, the angle and force of impact, the final gestural movement, final lip and eye movement, blood smears and bruised stains, the bones crumpled. What intensities were emitted? What sparks? The curvature and folding of the line of flight, the distorted wailing moan, the neighbor's dog barking, the elongated and yellowed fingernails splattered with blood, the organs ruptured and heaving, the sheen of sweat on his forehead, motionless, the flesh drooping from the bones, in pendulous tension, his shoe half on, a slithery trickle of blood coalescing, grey light reflecting in the distance, intense motionlessness, the final ebb of muscles, the heavy wind momentarily shuddering, then evanescing, his jacket collar fluttering in the wind, the blood mingling with dirt on his knee. The body still, motionless, but all around, gripped by seething and shivering.

The world stares blankly on, indifferent, unperturbed, silently fixated, as yet unresolved. The crumpled manuscripts, 'le grandeur de Marx,' spilt on the carpet, fluttering in disarray, unfinished, rustle as a shimmering dizziness floated in the air.

"This idea of the fall implies no context of misery, failure or suffering... The fall is what is most alive in the sensation."[2] The fall is the passage of escape, the passage of sensation, the most intense and radical departure. Folding the line to the outside, folding it back inside, curled around, out manoeuvred, stretched till it breaks.

The final page, the crushing static, the unresolved and insufferable abandonment. "There are no deaths, only assassinations."[3] There are no Ends. First you trick life into existence, then you can play tricks with death. The immanence which is in nothing, is itself a life. We all wonder alone...

Notes

1   'Of the New Idol' in Nietzsche's *Thus Spoke Zarathustra* p. 77
2   Gilles Deleuze, Francis Bacon, *The Logic of Sensation*,
         Continuum, London, New York, 2003, p. 82
3   'R as in Resistance' from *Gilles Deleuze L'Abécédaire/From A to Z*

Robert Lort is an art critic, renowned performance poet and avant-garde music and film connoisseur. He has written on everything from Kathy Acker to Jean-Luc Godard to New York surveillance cameras to multi-media and performance art. His fiction and poetry and reviews have been published around the net and in print. He speaks multiple languages and is currently learning Japanese. Robert Lort originated the Azimute website, the contents of which were published by Enigmatic Ink in 2011.